Read & Enjoy!

Donna Finch Slaton 4-18-16

Hi Mason

I hope you enjoy this book!

A "storyteller" friend of your <u>great</u> grandparents!

Donna

"Miss Pockets"

Ben Beagle Plays

Written By
Donna Finch Slaton

Illustrated By
Donna Brooks

Heart to Heart Publishing, Inc.

Heart to Heart Publishing, Inc.
528 Mud Creek Road • Morgantown, KY 42261
(270) 526-5589
www.hearttoheartpublishinginc.com

Copyright © 2015
Publishing Rights: Heart to Heart Publishing, Inc.
Publishing Date January 2016
Library of Congress Control No. 2015952907
ISBN 978-1-937008-43-7

Author: Donna Finch Slaton
Artist: Donna Brooks
Editor: L.J.Gill
Copy-Editor: Susan Mitchell
Designer: April Yingling-Jernigan
Author Photo Credit: Gina Munger

Printed in USA

First Edition
10 9 8 7 6 5 4 3 2

There are hidden hearts throughout the pages of this book.

May seeking the heart pictures serve as a reminder that Heart to Heart Publishing
desires to touch hearts through reading good books.

Dedication

With a heart grateful to God, this book is dedicated to my family, our pets and all the children who attended storyhour or other programs I have done in the past 40 years. It is also dedicated to my first career role model, Virgie D. Kirk, Librarian of Concord Elementary School, Paducah, KY, who in 1963 led me to love the library.
~Donna Finch Slaton

4

Ben the beagle
lives on a farm

In a nice little dog house
to keep himself warm

His special area
included a tree

He would sit on a root,
look around and see

What and who was passing by

And talk to them, yes, he would try

BRRRRRRR!

BRRRRRRR!

BRRRRRRR!

Squirrel in the tree above,

Bird in the sky,

Family
coming in
and out
the door,

The cat washing
his leg and more,

The cardinal that flew high
away from the cat,

**The fat frog that jumped
in a puddle, splat!**

The wren that nested in the porch rafter,

The basset hound,
Frank, who caused
his people such
laughter,

18

The coonhounds, Katie and Kelly, in the pen,

Jumping and bouncing again and again.

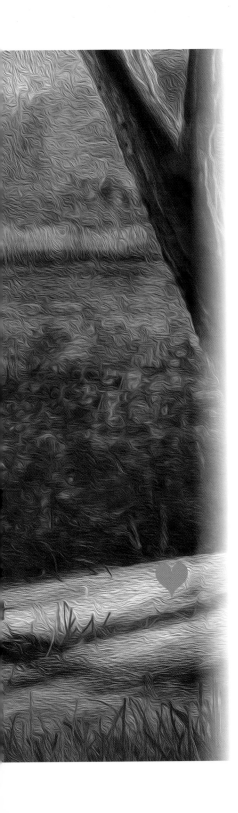

Just across the driveway
beyond truck and tractor

Was the play place that Ben
Beagle always longed after.

And each time he was released to play,
Straight to the thicket he ran first to say:
BRRRRR BRRRRR BRRRRR!

Somewhere inside that thicket you see,
was a rabbit munching as quiet as can be.

When
Ben went
BRRRRR
the rabbit
ran

and that was
when the
chase began.

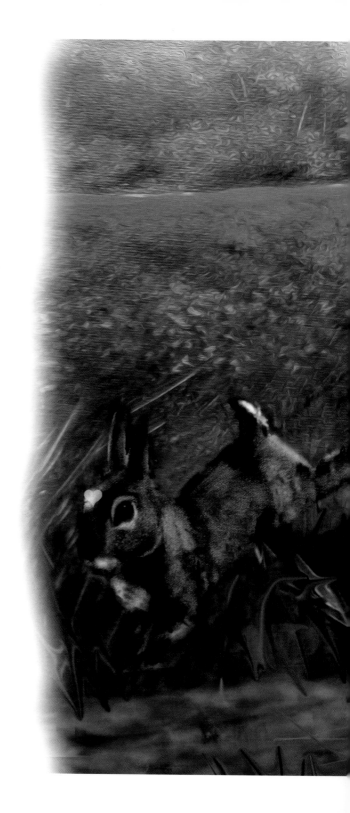

Beagles are hunters
by nature you see
So chasing rabbits
was meant to be.

Ben never catches; he only chases. His people love his joyful voice when he races.

BRRRRR, BRRRRR, BRRRRR!

When he comes home from a long run going in the kitchen for a treat is much fun.

Then, just like you, a cuddle in a chair

a nap with his people is Ben's to share!

Facts about Beagles

1. Beagles have been an American Kennel Club Registered breed since 1885.

2. Beagles may be 13-15 inches. 13 inches and under are called littles. Ben is a little beagle.

3. "Miss P" - 15 inches – a regular beagle, won the 2015 Westminster Dog Show, Best of Show, top dog honor.

4. Beagles are often pictured as black, tan and white, which is called tri-color, and they can be a variety of color combinations and also solid red, brown, black or tan.

5. Beagles are scent hounds and often run with their nose touching the ground.

6. Beagles do not need to be trained to hunt, it is their nature.

7. Beagles do need to be trained to return to their humans and respond to calls and commands, but even when trained, if on a hot rabbit trail, the beagle will be difficult to call home.

Memories of Ben Beagle

1. Where does Ben cuddle when he is done playing?

2. Where does Ben live?

3. What kind of dog is his friend Frank?

4. What are the names of the coonhound twins?

5. What are some other animals in the yard?

6. What kind of birds are in the story?

7. Who does Ben chase when he runs?

8. Where does he go to hunt and race?

9. Where does he go to get dog food and treats?

10. Which words in the story start with "tr"?

1. a lap
2. a farm
3. Basset Hound
4. Katie & Kelly
5. cat, squirrel, frog
6. wren, cardinal, goldfinch
7. rabbit
8. thicket
9. kitchen
10. tree, truck, tractor, treat

Hidden Hearts

Page 4-5: Beans & Collar (2)
Page 6-7: On tree (1)
Page 8: Collar (1)
Page 10: In tree (1)
Page 11: Wing (1)
Page 12: First toe of shoe (1)
Page 13: On paw (1)
Page 14: Wing (1)
Page 15: Back leg of frog (1)
Page 16: On right side (1)
Page 17: Tip of tail (1)
Page 18: Below pen (1)
Page 19: Below pen (1)
Page 20 & 21: Road (1)
Page 22: Beside front paw (1)
Page 23: In Rabbit's eye (1)
Page 24 & 25: Rabbit's forehead, pasture (2)
Page 26 & 27: Rabbit's forehead, pasture (2)
Page 28: In tree (1)
Page 29: Hanging on porch, wall paper border, on table (7)
Page 30: On man's chest (1)

Total: 30